FROM the BugaBees SERIES

the BugyBops
friends for all time

by Amy Recob

Illustrated by 64 Colors

BEAVER'S POND
PRESS

ISBN 10: 1-59298-474-6
ISBN 13: 978-1-59298-474-9

Library of Congress Catalog Number: 2012905355
Printed in the United States of America
First Printing: 2012
16 15 14 13 12   5 4 3 2 1

Cover and interior design by 64 Colors

Beaver's Pond Press, Inc.
7108 Ohms Lane
Edina, MN 55439-2129
(952) 829-8818
www.BeaversPondPress.com

To order, visit www.BeaversPondBooks.com or call (800) 901-3480.
Reseller discounts available.

BugaBees® is a registered trademark of Moxie Creations, LLC.

**To Maxwell Scott,
The most precious
BugyBop of all**

For more information, visit www.thebugabees.com.

Some of the scenarios portrayed in this book may not be applicable to
all food allergies. Allergic reactions and their severity, preventive measures,
and emergency treatments can all vary greatly depending on the individual and the
level of food-allergen exposure. Always talk to those affected by food allergies about the most
appropriate course of action for their situations.

This is a story for all BugyBops—
When they get together the fun never stops!

These kindhearted friends are on hand to show
Some lifesaving tips so you, too, can know
Just how to help the BugaBees, their favorite buggy friends,
Who all live with food allergies and things called EpiPens.

These special shots of medicine they must bring everywhere.
Certain foods can make them sick, so they take extra care
Not to eat or touch the foods that they're allergic to,
But EpiPens can save their lives if they accidentally do.

No peanuts (please!) for Cricket, for Dragonfly no soy,
And eating foods containing milk makes Beetle one sick boy.

No fish for little Ladybug, no eggs for Bumblebee,
For Firefly no tree nuts from the corner bakery.
For Butterfly no shellfish, for Caterpillar no wheat,
But even without all these foods, their friendships still stay sweet!

The BugyBops do all they can to help the BugaBees,
Like wash their hands, and choose safe foods, and never ever tease.
And in case of an emergency, BugyBops know what to say—
"Our friend is sick, we need some help, find a grown-up right away!"

Since getting sick from certain foods is really no vacation,
The BugyBops help stop the spread of cross-contamination.
Then foods like peanut butter, which can stick to hands and faces,
Won't rub off on desks, or books, or toys, or other unwanted places.

So just in case, the BugyBops keep these foods far away
When BugaBees will be around, so they can safely play.
They always ask ahead of time which foods will be all right
To snack on when the BugaBees come camp out overnight.

On field trips, when they get to go someplace they've never been,
The BugyBops remind their friends to bring their medicine.
They help their pals remember they should take it when they leave,
In fanny packs or in book bags, or even up their sleeve.

On holidays throughout the year—January to December—
When choosing special foods to share, the BugyBops remember...

To pick out treats their friends can eat by always reading labels
And keep those goodies safe to eat at separate party tables.

The BugyBops and BugaBees have so much fun together,
In rain or shine, in hot or cold, in calm or stormy weather.
Their kindness shows in all they do—food allergies or not—
Because their friendship means the most, and that means quite a lot!

So if you have a friend or two, a sibling, or a classmate
With allergies like BugaBees, there are ways to make them feel great.
Be kind to them and help them out, just like the BugyBops,
And if you do, this much is true: your friendship will be tops!

BugyBops
Activities & Talking Points

Millions of children are living with food allergies all throughout the world, and the number of diagnosed cases increases each year. While the medical community works to find a cure, the care and support of friends and family are essential in managing and preventing allergic reactions.

Knowing what symptoms to watch for, which foods to avoid, and what precautions to take are all key factors in successfully helping others to minimize the risks associated with food allergies.

While BugyBop characters are intended to provide general guidelines for helping children manage food allergies, it is important to acknowledge that not all food allergies are alike. Allergic reactions and their severity, preventive measures, and emergency treatments can all vary greatly depending on the individual and the level of food-allergen exposure. Always talk to those affected by food allergies about the most appropriate course of action for their situations.

Are you a BugyBop Kid?

Read the following pages and learn how to:

K Keep all kids safe from food allergens

I Inform others about food allergies

D Develop friendships for a lifetime!

THROAT, EYES & NOSE SYMPTOMS
Raspy voice, tightness, hoarseness, trouble with swallowing, itchy or watery eyes, runny nose

MOUTH SYMPTOMS
Itchy mouth, swelling lips or tongue

STOMACH SYMPTOMS
Cramps, aches, pains, vomiting, diarrhea

KNOW THE SIGNS OF AN ALLERGIC REACTION

SKIN SYMPTOMS
Itchy red bumps, hives, rashes, swelling, blue or pale color

HEART SYMPTOMS
Dizziness, weak pulse, feeling faint or confused

LUNG SYMPTOMS
Coughing, wheezing, trouble with breathing

Did you know...

The BugaBees represent the eight most common food allergies? They are:

• Peanuts   • Tree Nuts   • Fish   • Shellfish   • Milk   • Soy   • Eggs   • Wheat

BugyBops
do all they can to help

Keep all kids safe from food allergens.

See if you know some of the simple ways you, too, can protect a life:

1. BugyBops choose safe foods by reading ingredient labels and asking the BugaBees ahead of time which treats are safe to share.
TRUE – or – FALSE?

2. When BugaBees are near, BugyBops keep foods that might be dangerous for their friends safely put away.
TRUE – or – FALSE?

3. BugyBops help the BugaBees remember to bring their medicine wherever they go.
TRUE – or – FALSE?

Answers: 1. True   2. True   3. True

BugyBops Bonus Tips:

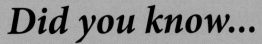

Did you know...

that food allergens can hide in the most unexpected places?

For example, there can be peanuts and tree nuts listed on labels for things like carrots and dip, pancake mix, or fruit snacks.

Eggs can often be found in some brands of taffy, and wheat can be found in some brands of licorice.

Sometimes different package sizes for the same exact type of food can have different allergy warnings, based on where they were made.

Food allergens can also be found in things like shampoo, lotion, pet food, gardening supplies, and more. Never assume a product is safe unless you've read its label — each and every time!

BugyBops
do all they can to help

Inform others about food allergies.

See if you know some of the simple ways you, too, can teach friends and family about food safety:

1. BugyBops remind others to wash their hands after eating to help stop the spread of cross-contamination.
TRUE – or – FALSE?

2. If a BugaBee gets sick from eating or touching a certain food, BugyBops always tell a grown-up immediately in case of an emergency.
TRUE – or – FALSE?

3. BugyBops explain to others that doctors and nurses use EpiPens in hospitals to write detailed notes about medication for their patients.
TRUE – or – FALSE?

Answers: 1. True   2. True   3. False

BugyBops Bonus Tips:

Did you know...

that EpiPens are *not* the kind of pens you write with?
They contain special shots of medicine called epinephrine.
In case of an emergency, EpiPen shots can be given directly
through clothing into a person's upper thigh.

EpiPens should be used within three minutes of an allergic reaction.
Once injected, the medicine works for about twenty
minutes, so it's a good idea to always have an extra one
on hand. Be sure to call a doctor or an ambulance right
after an EpiPen has been used.

EpiPens should be keep at room-temperature
and never stored in a cold fridge, freezer
or hot car.

BugyBops
do all they can to help

Develop friendships for a lifetime!

See if you know some of the simple ways you, too, can be a great friend:

1. BugyBops help BugaBees feel included at special parties and other activities by choosing safe foods to share.
TRUE – or – FALSE?

2. If a BugaBee feels sad or scared because of foods others are eating, BugyBops think about how they would feel in the same situation and try to help their friend.
TRUE – or – FALSE?

3. BugyBops show kindness and respect to the BugaBees and to everyone, even people who have different needs and abilities other than their own.
TRUE – or – FALSE?

Answers: 1. True   2. True   3. True

BugyBops Bonus Tips:

Did you know...

that kindness and understanding are some of the best gifts you can give to a friend?

Everyone feels sad, scared, or disappointed sometimes, but the caring support of others can make all the difference.

With a little extra planning and consideration, it's easy to help friends with food allergies stay safe and still have lots of fun!

Caring about others inspires others to care about you, and that's one of the very best ways you can develop friendships for a lifetime!

The End